RALPH
and the Rocket Ship

by Alyssa Satin Capucilli ★ illustrated by Henry Cole

Ready-to-Read

Simon Spotlight

New York London Toronto Sydney New Delhi

For Stella Hazel and Dylan Lazarus,
my newest stars!
—A. S. C.

For H. R. G.
—H. C.

SIMON SPOTLIGHT
An imprint of Simon & Schuster Children's Publishing Division
1230 Avenue of the Americas, New York, New York 10020
This Simon Spotlight edition September 2016

For information about special discounts for bulk purchases, please contact Simon & Schuster Special Sales at 1-866-506-1949 or business@simonandschuster.com.
Manufactured in the United States of America 0816 LAK
10 9 8 7 6 5 4 3 2 1
This book has been cataloged with the Library of Congress.
ISBN 978-1-4814-5866-5 (pbk)
ISBN 978-1-4814-5867-2 (hc)
ISBN 978-1-4814-5868-9 (eBook)

This is Ralph.

Ralph loves things that go fast!

Ralph loves cars.

He loves trains and trucks.

Most of all,
he loves rocket ships.

One day, Ralph asked
for a rocket ship.

“A rocket ship can take me up to the stars,” said Ralph.

“A rocket ship can take me to the moon!” he said.

“A rocket ship can take me
to planets far, far away!
Zip! Zoom! Whoosh!”

“A rocket ship is too big,”

said Ralph’s mother.

“Here is your train.”

“Choo! Choo! Chug!”
Ralph’s train could not
reach the stars.

“A rocket ship is too tall,”
said his father.
“Here is your tractor.”

“Clink! Clank! Clunk!”
Ralph’s tractor could not
fly to the moon.

“There must be some way
to get a rocket ship,”
said Ralph.

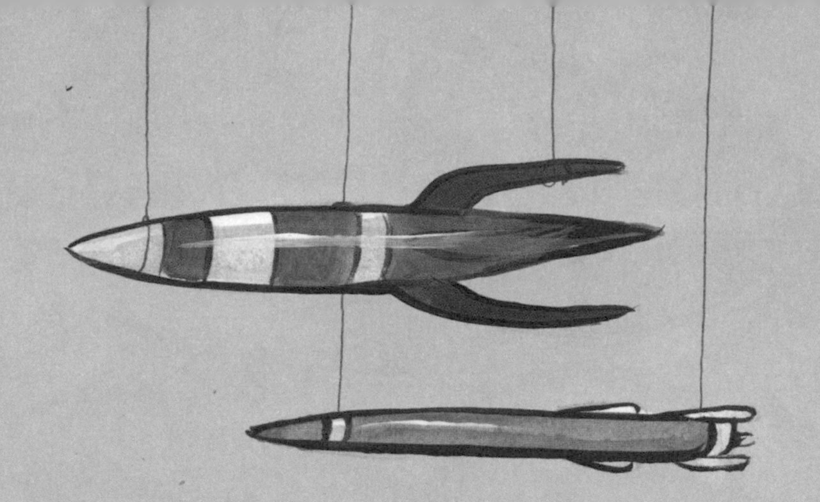

"Zip! Zoom! Whoosh!

But how?"

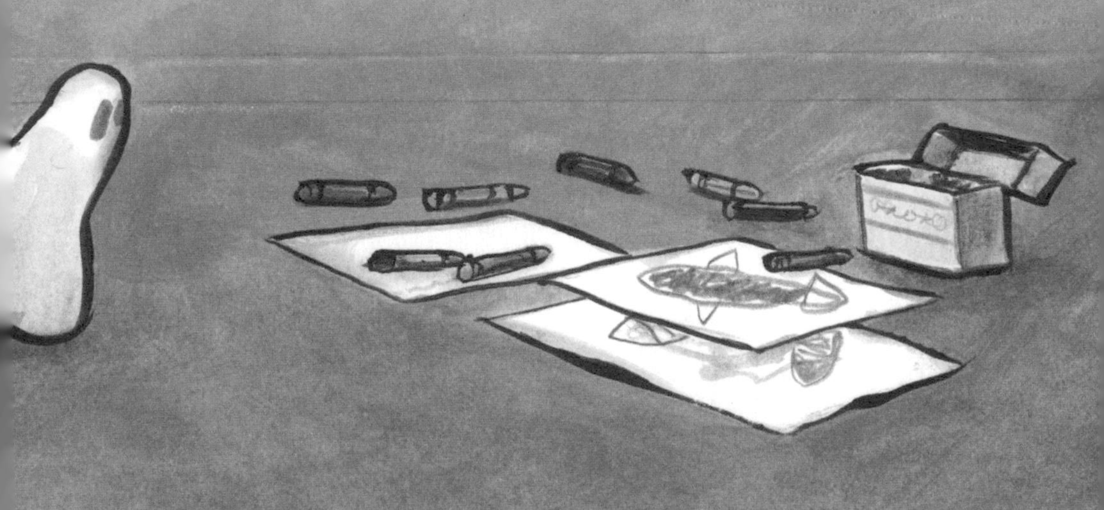

Ralph thought and thought.

He thought some more.

And then . . .

Stack!

Stack!

Tap!

Tap!

Bang! Bang!

Tape, tape, tape, tape!

"10-9-8-7-6-5-4-3-2-1 . . .

Blast off!" shouted Ralph.

Ralph's rocket ship went up
to the stars, and the moon,
and the faraway planets.

Ralph's rocket ship took him wherever he wanted to go.

"Zip! Zoom! Whoosh!"

And there was
plenty of room
for his friend Katy too.